Roar's Strumming,
Let's Get
Humming!

Hazel Reev

Illustrated by Dave

This is Roar,
the little dinosaur.

"Roar, roar, roar!
I'm a little dinosaur.
I love swaying,
let's get playing."

Roar is brave
and Roar is strong.
She often likes
to sing a song.

"Fill my bag up,
shake maracas!
Lots of instruments,
cheese and crackers."

Roar likes strumming
like a rock star.
Thinks of driving
in a big car.

"Daddy's strumming
very bravely.
How I love
my ukulele!"

Roar is marching
to the drum beat.
Up and down
she stamps her green feet.

"Tappety, tap, tap —
this is fun!
Louder! Louder!
Crash that drum!"

Roar loves hand bells
in a line.
Conducts her friend
to stay in time.

"Red and yellow,
green and blue.
Ring the bells
for me and you."

Roar can play notes
high and low.
On the piano,
watch her go.

"Jingly, jangly,
off I go.
Playing fast
and playing slow."

Roar likes singing
with a friend.
Repeating songs
that never end.

"I am happy
and I know it.
Come on, friend,
you've got to show it."

Roar, where are you?

Roar makes music
in the shed.
Counting quietly
in her head.

"1, 2, 3,
4, 5, 6.
Playing flowerpots
with my sticks."

Roar loves dancing
to the flute.
Feel the rhythm,
tap your boot.

"Country dancing
round and round.
Lift my friend up
off the ground."

Roar can blow
her little trumpet.
Calls her friend
to eat some crumpet.

"Rooty tooty,
let's eat tea.
One for you
and one for me."

Roar's rehearsing
for a show.
With her friend,
a song they know.

"Twinkle, twinkle,
little star.
My friend's playing
her guitar."

Roar loves bath-time,
pouring, filling.
Plays the bottles
and starts singing.

"Funny noises
from the bath tub.
Blowing, tapping,
sinking, glub, glub."

Roar likes singing
about her day.
Composing songs
that she can play.

"La, la, la,
Ding-a-ling!
I can play
and I can sing."

Roar likes bed-time,
time to sing.
Giving Grandma
a bell to ring.

Grandma peers
around the door.
Sings a song
for little Roar.

Other Roar books available from LDA are:

Hello, Roar, Little Dinosaur (*intended to introduce Roar to children*)
Come on Roar, Let's Explore!
Roar's Creating, Let's Get Making!
Roar's In Shorts, Let's Play Sports!
Roar's About, Let's Go Out!

The rights of Hazel Reeves and Dave McTaggart to be identified as the authors of this work have been asserted by them in accordance with sections 77 and 78 of the Copyright, Designs and Patents Act 1988.

Roar's Strumming, Let's Get Humming!

ISBN: 978-1-85503-539-3

© Hazel Reeves and Dave McTaggart

First published 2013

Printed in the UK for LDA

LDA, Findel Education, Hyde Buildings, Ashton Road, Hyde, Cheshire, SK14 4SH